THE REVENGE OF JIMMY

A SCARY GODMOTHER STORY
written and illustrated by
JILL THOMPSON
SIRIUS ENTERTAINMENT

Robb Horan
Publisher

Larry Salamone
President

Joseph Michael Linsner
Art Director

Mark Bellis
Managing Editor

McNabb Studios
Production

Digital Logo Design
Joseph Allen

Book Design
Jill Thompson

ISBN# 1-57989-020-2
Thompson, Jill
SCARY GODMOTHER / THE REVENGE OF JIMMY / by Jill Thompson

Summary: To save himself from the monsters that roam the earth on Halloween, Jimmy tries to stop the holiday from happening.

Printed by Brenner Printing
San Antonio, Texas
USA

SCARY GODMOTHER – THE REVENGE OF JIMMY Vol. One. First Printing, September 1998.
Published by Sirius Entertainment, Inc. Correspondence: PO Box 834, Dover, NJ 07802.

dedicated
to
Emma
and
Elizabeth

If there was one thing **Jimmy** knew about – it was **MONSTERS**! He quivered with fear each day after school since the month of October began!

You see, monsters are free to roam the world each and every Halloween. They lurk in the shadows waiting to gobble up the **tastiest** of snacks – mischievous boys and girls – and Jimmy was sure they would be **coming to get him**.

Last Halloween, Jimmy and his gang had **barely escaped** the clutches of a giant, toothy horror! But the monster had a **taste** for him now, and in a matter of days it would be back— **under every** staircase and **behind every** door!

Since then, Jimmy had taken every precaution to prevent monsters from getting to him! He **slept** with the lights on...

He kept a good supply of **flashlights** on hand at all times (monsters hate light)...

He made sure there was **no room** under his bed for monsters...

He **cleaned** out his closet...

And he never–ever–**EVER** went into the basement!

But on Halloween, monsters could go **wherever** they wanted! Clearly, he was doomed, rules were rules! Jimmy thought and thought until his head was sore!

Hearing his parents gave Jimmy an **idea**!

A **nasty, mean, selfish** and **devilish** idea!

On the other side of town, Jimmy's little cousin **Hannah Marie**, couldn't wait for Halloween!

She **used to be** afraid of the dark and the things that went bump in the night; but she had a **Scary Godmother** who knew all about spooky things and she shared her spectral secrets with the little girl! Hannah's fears "poofed" away and Halloween became her **favorite** holiday!

Over on the Fright Side, we're **always** gettin' ready for Halloween—it's what we're all about! But, you know how crazy stuff gets at the **last minute**! You should see the **commotion** goin' on at the Scary Godmother's house!

She's cookin' up **potions** and bottling **frights**! Capturin' **shrieks** an' paintin' **clouds** into the night! An' when every Autumn leave is crisped and shivers chill your bones—she gathers up the **Boozle** 'cause their work has just begun!

Her little bat wings lift her **high** into the sky, so she can better round up **rascals** for their favorite, frightening night!

Restless **souls** and **spirits** soar silently an' sigh as giggling, ghoulish **ghosties** gang up as if to **fight**! Rousted by the Boozle, they take off in spectral flight!

Through cobweb coated corridors our spooky fairy flies! She'll wake the **undead King** and **Queen**, who slumber in their coffins and dream of **bloody** things.

Once they are awakened, an **ice-cold mist** appears! It cushions vampire footsteps and allows them to draw near! In regal, nightmare velvet they float up the marble stair, with fantastic, flapping fanfare to join the **dark affair**...

Creatures **bubble** from the ponds an' streams and **foam** out from the Sea...

While others grumble out from **under hills** and drop down from the trees...

Standing on a hilltop with the **moon** so **shiny bright**...

Special **magic** words fly out like **bats** into the night!

A carved and stony bridge takes form an' stretches far an' wide...

To carry nightmare creatures away from the Fright Side!

So if you are out **Treatin'**, or playin' a **Trick** or two...keep an eye peeled for a monster—they're out waiting for **YOU!**

Bug-A-Boo's poem inspired Hannah at the dinner table.

Jimmy's mom was also inspired by Halloween — much to his dismay!

The next day, **everyone** discussed their plans for Halloween. The whole school was crazy for it! **Except** Jimmy.

He spent his time formulating his elaborate anti-Halloween plot!

And when his parents thought he was snug in his bed, Jimmy **crept** out into the deep, dark night to set his plan in motion!

16

At that **exact** moment, a thick soup of **fog** poured all over the Fright side!

And try as she might..

The Scary Godmother **couldn't** lead the way to the Halloween Bridge!

The next morning when people came to buy their pumpkins, they found the pumpkin farm was **closed**! But why? Hannah rattled the gate until the farmer came over.

A cloud of disappointment settled over the crowd and Jimmy felt triumphant...

...**until** little Emma spoke up!

The Anderson farm sold **all** of their pumpkins that day...

...and Jimmy sulked home to plan another dastardly deed!

The blanket of cold, clammy fog --"**POOF**"--disappeared and the bridge to Halloween was again free and clear!

Porches and windows sported toothsome, new **jack-o-lanterns**...

...that leered at Jimmy as he snuck back into the night!

The next afternoon when people showed up to buy their Halloween costumes, they were greeted by Jimmy's nasty handiwork. **All** the costumes were **stamped**...

Jimmy's fingers clawed in the air while he danced with hunchbacked glee.

A **net** had stretched, silky and strong across the Fright Side sky! It hung over the trees and draped across the monsters' houses.

It **could not** be burned, or snipped, or broken...

And it **trapped** them on the other side of Halloween!

Daryl and Bert got to talking...

And the weird web **withered** and was **whisked** away by the cinnamon wind!

Jimmy's nostrils snuffed up gulps of cool, autumn air as he passed houses bustling with costume creation! He **grumbled** at them on his way to commit mischief...

Jimmy could hardly contain his glee when everyone came to the candy store to stock up for **Trick or Treats**.

The thought of Halloween **without candy** caused a salty torrent to flow from the children's sad eyes.

Thunder rumbled in the inky clouds that hung in the Fright Side sky. **BOOM HOO HOO!**
The sky sobbed furiously—casting down sheets of stormy tears!

A raging river rushed through the hills and the valleys, rousting monsters out of their crypts
and caves. It swept them up the stairs to the tippy top of the Scary Godmother's house!

The flash flood fled as suddenly as it came, leaving the forests of the Fright Side decked out with **drippy-droppy** jewels!

Jimmy had **one night** left to stop Halloween from coming, but he'd **already** run through his list of monster stopping tricks! What to do...What to do...?

27

He worked **all through** the night...

And was **back in his bed** by the time his mother came in to check on him!

It was **Halloween Day**! Hip, Hip, **HOORAY**! Brightly colored **leaves** scuttled past children dressed in **fine**, **homemade** costumes, **vainly competing** for some kind of attention! Ghoulish, little girls and teeny, tiny terrors rushed past storybook mermaids and transistor robots—all **masquerading** their way to school!

Copious amounts of **cupcakes** were consumed in classroom parties.

And after school it was **ding-dong ditch** and **target practice** for every door!

Late Halloween afternoon, Jimmy crept out of his 'sick' bed to see the heartache his handiwork had caused. He **spied** on the parade volunteers and gargled with glee!

Meanwhile, the monsters merrily made their way toward the Halloween Bridge decked out in their finest Nightmare-Wear!

The main streets were **lined** with people who waited for a parade that would never arrive! Hannah waited and waited, until she could **wait no more**!

Betty pulled Hannah towards the fieldhouse and the crowd soon followed along.

The children were the first to arrive.

The FLOATS are RUINED!

There won't be any PARADE!

HALLOWEEN is RUINED!

Thick, varicose vines **twiggled** out of the earth and **obscured** the Halloween Bridge! The intestinal innards reached way into the sky—they even went **higher** than the Scary Godmother could fly!

A wild, warm wind whispered all around them, drying their salty tears!

OH! LOOK AT THE FLOATS!

THEY'RE GHOSTS! BEAUTIFUL, GIANT-SIZED GHOSTIES! DON'T YOU SEE?

THAT'S A SKULLY MAN GHOST...

AND THAT'S A PUN'KIN GHOST!

AND THERE'S SPIDER LADY and WITCH GHOSTS!

WHICH GHOST?

HA HA! THE ONE IN THE CORNER!

AND EVEN A GHOST GHOST!

The crowd "**oohed**" and "**aahed**" as Hannah explained.

And with **that**, the terrible tower of thorns toppled and Halloween **busted out** all over! A cavalcade of creatures flew high with kids and floats in tow! Real ghosts glided overhead in an ectoplasmic show!

Mister Pettibone clacked and the monsters **mashed** to the light of a magical fire!

Jimmy **puffed up** with pride, like a marshmallow in the microwave! He **clawed** his way into the clearing and **belted** out in a baritone bark—

Jimmy had become **so horrible**, he **scared** even **Bug-A-Boo!**

Jimmy pulled with all of his might, but he wasn't heavy enough to weigh down the balloon!

And the monsters he had feared **did not** gobble him up. They **helped** him to **save** the Halloween his deeds made...

Safe on the ground, Jimmy glowed with **gratitude**.

THANK YOU FOR SAVING ME AND MY BALLOON!

PUT 'ER THERE!

GOOD JOB, KID

YOU GAVE ME A **GREAT SCARE!** I'LL HAVE TO CHECK UNDER **MY** BED TO SEE IF **YOU** MIGHT BE THERE!

HA!

THAT WOULD BE SCARY!

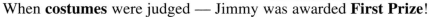

When **costumes** were judged — Jimmy was awarded **First Prize**!

THAT **DR. JEKYL** AND **MR. HYDE** COSTUME WAS AMAZING!

I JUST **WISH** I **HADN'T** RUINED ALL OF THAT CANDY....

IT'S THE **ONLY** PART OF HALLOWEEN THAT **DIDN'T** GET FIXED!!

39

Haunting, soft music blew from out of the trees! Jimmy ran **lickety-split** so he was the first one to see the magical sight!

There were enough **treat**s for **everyone** with plenty left over! All the folks agreed, it was the best **Halloween** that they could remember! And for Jimmy, **revenge** certainly was **sweet**!

The End